Aesop's Fables
The Hare and the Tortoise

Miles Kelly

The hare was always boasting about how fast he could run. "I'm the fastest animal in the land," he would say.

One day the hare asked, "Who will run a race against me?"

The other animals were fed up with the hare's boasting, but no one would accept his challenge for fear of losing...

...no one except the tortoise.

"Ha ha!"

The hare laughed out loud. The other animals gasped.

The tortoise just smiled.

Preparations for the race began. The fox drew up a map of the route. The race was to take place the following week.

Whoosh!

For the next seven days the hare showed off, speeding around the meadow, dashing up hills, knocking animals over and upsetting just about everyone.

The tortoise just watched from afar as he chewed leisurely on grass and leaves.

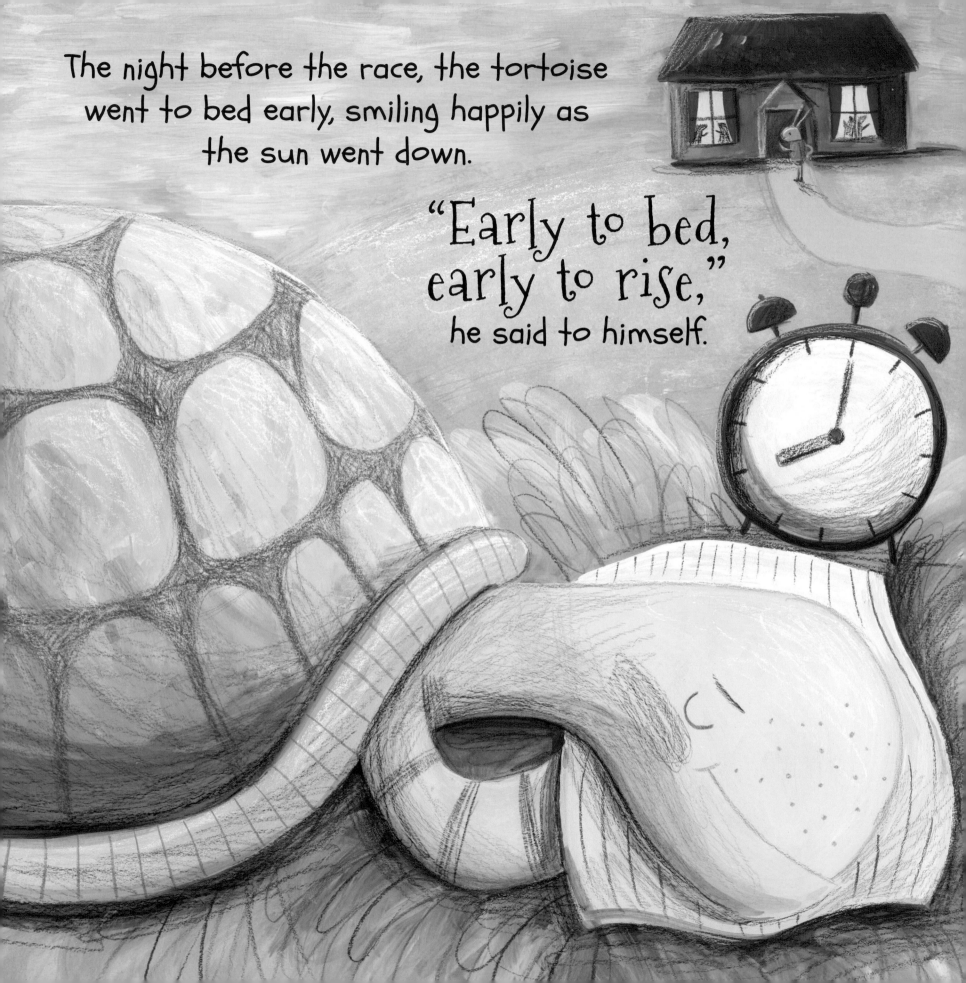

The night before the race, the tortoise went to bed early, smiling happily as the sun went down.

"Early to bed, early to rise," he said to himself.

SHHH!

Meanwhile, the hare stayed up late, partying with his neighbours, the badgers.

Their **noisy** antics kept everyone awake.

The next day dawned **bright and sunny.**

The tortoise awoke refreshed and full of energy. He ate a hearty breakfast then got ready for the race.

The hare wasn't feeling quite so refreshed. His late night meant he had hardly slept at all. He felt **exhausted.**

He poured himself a large glass of carrot juice and yawned loudly.

Out in the meadow, the animals were gathering for the race.

There were stalls selling cakes and sandwiches. Balloons and bunting had been tied to trees.

A party atmosphere was building!

At last it was time
for the race to start.

Feeling more like his usual
self, the hare took his place
at the start line.
"Get ready to lose!"
he said to the tortoise.

The tortoise just smiled. He didn't seem in the least bit worried.

Then the fox began the countdown to the race.

"On your marks... Get set..."
The whistle blew, and they were off!

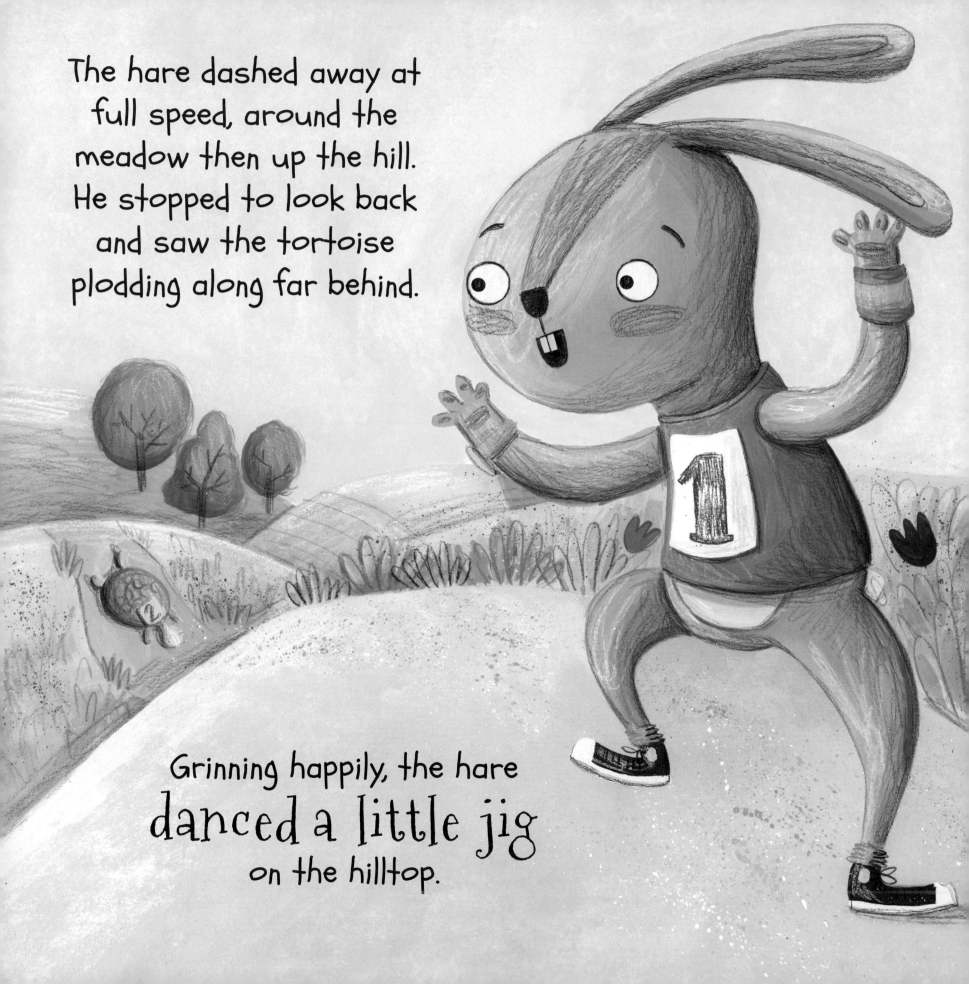

The hare dashed away at full speed, around the meadow then up the hill. He stopped to look back and saw the tortoise plodding along far behind.

Grinning happily, the hare danced a little jig on the hilltop.

As he ran down the hill, the hare grabbed some crunchy lettuces from a field. He stopped for a mid-morning snack.

Yummy!

The sun was warm and he decided to have a short nap. After all, he'd had a late night, and the tortoise was far behind.

In the meantime, the tortoise carried on, up the hill and over the top.

ZZZZZ

He saw the hare snoozing
under a tree, and marched
bravely past.

The hare didn't stir a whisker.

Much, much later, feeling stiff and cold, the hare woke up with a start.

He looked up at the sun and saw how low it was in the sky. It must be almost evening! He feared the worst.

With the finish line in sight and the crowd roaring him on, the tortoise staggered on as fast as he could.

A few minutes later he crossed the line to huge applause and the crowd shouting his name.

The hare had lost his own challenge.

From now on perhaps he wouldn't be so boastful.

Slow and steady wins the race.